19/-

10^e

.P

RAY BRADBURY CHRONICLES

I
The April Witch

II
Trapdoor

III
Picasso Summer

NANTIER • BEALL • MINOUSTCHINE
publishing inc.
new york

A BYRON PREISS VISUAL PUBLICATIONS, INC. BOOK

INTRODUCTION

One must be on the alert, always. It matters not what areas of life you're in. Things are always creeping up on you; ideas, hidden in the underbrush, wallow to be born. Sometimes they hit you over the head with a rubber hammer. Sometimes they hit you in the face with a fake lemon pie. On occasion you walk on them.

The problem is, most people are clever at avoiding ideas. They duck and weave and refuse to be crept up on. They pretend not to notice that a rubber hammer has hit them or that they are walking right across a notion, fancy, or concept.

My business is letting the pie hit me square on. And since I am always looking down, watchful for hopscotch pentagrams or snails, I surprise myself with lalapaloozin' story ideas. Take "Picasso Summer," for instance . . .

I was walking on the beach with my wife and several friends, thirty-six years ago, and picked up a Popsicle stick and started to draw in the wet sand. As I drew, I said, "Wouldn't it be something to be walking along the beach in Southern France and meet up with Picasso drawing his fabulous mythological beasts on the shore?" "Wow!" I added, and cried: "Gimme a pencil, someone!" My wife handed me a pad and pencil and I wrote down the opening of "Picasso Summer."

"Trapdoor" was another surprise hidden out in the open and waiting. My wife and I moved into our new home with our four daughters thirty-five years ago. We were in the house for some ten years before I noticed a trapdoor in one of the ceilings. My gosh, I thought, has that trapdoor been there all these years? How come I didn't notice? And what's behind the trapdoor, up there in the unseen attic? Bam! I wrote the story that night. You could write it, too. Just climb up a ladder in your house and open the trapdoor (if you have one) and stick your head in . . .

"The April Witch" was much longer in arriving. It's the sort of idea you imagine when you are five, eight or twelve—or seventy-three, if you are me. We all like to wonder about how it feels to be a dog, a cat, a hummingbird, or a whale. I couldn't stand it any longer, imagining such things, so I created a wondrous girl-woman, Cecy, and let her fly about, ricochetting through the minds and looking out the eyes of frogs, crickets, sparrows, great danes, cows, and—other young women like herself. In no time at all, a few hours, "April Witch" was born. Pop inside it and look out through Cecy's eyes!

Ray Bradbury

Jon J Muth is an acknowledged master of the painted graphic novel. His work in this area includes *Moonshadow* and *Havok & Wolverine—Meltdown* for Marvel/Epic, *Dracula—A Symphony in Moonlight and Nightmares* for NBM, *The Mythology Of An Abandoned City* for Tundra, and *Fritz Lang's M* for Eclipse comics. He is currently working with Grant Morrison on a new graphic novel called *The Mystery Play*. "The April Witch" is one of his favorite stories.

John Van Fleet's credits include illustrations for various Topps trading cards (including the *Star Wars* and *Jurassic Park* card sets) and Clive Barker's *Primal* for Dark Horse Comics. He is currently working with John Rieber on a six-part story for DC's Vertigo line entitled *Shadows Fall*, due out spring 1994. John's work has been featured in galleries throughout the eastern United States.

John Ney Rieber's credits include authoring the novels *The Gates of the Night* and *Some are Angels*. His graphic novel scripts include *Tell Me, Dark*, his collaboration with author Karl Edward Wagner and artist Kent Williams, and *Shadows Fall* with John Van Fleet, both for DC comics.

Ross MacDonald was born on an air force base in Canada and moved to New York City to pursue his career as a professional illustrator. A lifetime comics fan, Ross's work has been strongly influenced by comics art, the work of Jack Kirby in particular. Ross's work has appeared in *Newsweek*, *The New York Times Magazine*, *Esquire*, *New York*, and many other magazines worldwide. Recently, he painted the covers for the reprint line of the novels of John Steinbeck. Ross also designed stage sets for the award-winning Broadway musical *Tommy*.

Cover by Jon J Muth
Frontispiece by Moebius
Colored by Dean Motter

THE APRIL WITCH
Adapted by Jon J Muth
Lettered by Rocky Ball

TRAPDOOR
Adapted by Ross MacDonald
Lettered by Willie Schubert

PICASSO SUMMER
Script by John Ney Rieber
Art by John Van Fleet
Lettered by Stephen Blue

Executive Editor: Byron Preiss
Editor: Howard Zimmerman
Art Director/Designer: Dean Motter
Assistant Editor: Kenneth Grobe

For imformation address:
Byron Preiss Visual Publications, Inc
24 West 25th Street , New York , New York 10010

Printed in Canada

The April Witch

INTO THE AIR, OVER THE VALLEYS, UNDER THE STARS, ABOVE A RIVER, A POND, A ROAD, CECY FLEW. INVISIBLE AS NEW SPRING WINDS, SHE SOARED IN DOVES, STOPPED IN TREES AND LIVED IN BLOSSOMS. SHE LIVED IN NEW APRIL GRASSES, IN SWEET CLEAR LIQUIDS RISING FROM THE MUSKY EARTH.

"IT'S SPRING. I'LL BE IN EVERY LIVING THING IN THE WORLD TONIGHT."

HERS WAS AN ADAPTABLY QUICK MIND FLOWING UNSEEN UPON ILLINOIS WINDS ON THIS ONE EVENING OF HER LIFE WHEN SHE WAS SEVENTEEN.

"I WANT TO BE IN LOVE."

SHE HAD SAID IT AT SUPPER. "PATIENCE," HAD BEEN HER PARENT'S ADVICE. "REMEMBER, YOU'RE REMARKABLE. WE CAN'T MIX OR MARRY WITH ORDINARY FOLK. WE'D LOSE OUR MAGICAL POWERS IF WE DID. YOU'D LOSE YOUR ABILITY TO *TRAVEL* BY MAGIC... SO, *BE CAREFUL!*

BUT IN HER HIGH BEDROOM, CECY HAD TOUCHED PERFUME TO HER THROAT AND STRETCHED OUT, TREMBLING AND APPREHENSIVE, ON HER FOUR-POSTER AS A MOON ROSE OVER ILLINOIS COUNTRY.

"I'M ONE OF AN ODD FAMILY. WE SLEEP DAYS AND FLY NIGHTS LIKE BLACK KITES ON THE WIND. IF WE WANT, WE CAN SLEEP IN MOLES THROUGH THE WINTER, IN THE WARM EARTH. I CAN LIVE IN ANYTHING AT ALL--A PEBBLE, A CROCUS, OR A PRAYING MANTIS. I CAN LEAVE MY PLAIN, BONY BODY BEHIND AND SEND MY MIND FAR OUT FOR ADVENTURE..."

"NOW!"

THE WIND WHIPPED HER OVER FIELDS AND MEADOWS.

OUTSIDE A FARMHOUSE IN THE SPRING NIGHT A DARK-HAIRED GIRL, NO MORE THAN NINE-TEEN, DREW UP WATER FROM A DEEP STONE WELL. SHE WAS SINGING. CECY FELL -- A GREEN LEAF -- INTO THE WELL.

SHE LAY IN THE TENDER MOSS OF THE WELL, GAZING UP THROUGH DARK COOLNESS. NOW IN A WATER DROPLET! AT LAST, WITHIN A COLD CUP. SHE FELT HERSELF LIFTED TO THE GIRL'S WARM LIPS. THERE WAS A SOFT NIGHT SOUND OF DRINKING. CECY LOOKED OUT FROM THE GIRL'S EYES.

WHO'S THERE?

"ONLY THE WIND."

ONLY THE WIND.

"WHAT'S YOUR NAME?"

ANN LEARY. NOW WHY SHOULD I SAY *THAT* OUT LOUD?

"ANN, ANN. ANN, YOU'RE GOING TO BE IN LOVE."

ANN!

IS THAT YOU, TOM?

WHO ELSE?

I'M NOT SPEAKING TO YOU!

NO!

LOOK WHAT YOU'VE DONE!

LOOK WHAT YOU *MADE* ME DO!

CECY YANKED A HIDDEN COPPER VENTRILOQUIST'S WIRE AND THE PRETTY MOUTH POPPED OPEN:

THANK YOU!

OH, SO YOU *HAVE* MANNERS?

NOT FOR YOU, NO!

I DON'T KNOW. I'VE GONE MAD. OH, GO AWAY!

HAVE YOU CHANGED YOUR MIND? WILL YOU GO WITH ME TO THE DANCE TONIGHT? IT'S SPECIAL. TELL YOU WHY LATER.

NO.

"YES! I'VE NEVER DANCED. I'VE NEVER WORN A LONG GOWN, ALL RUSTLY. I WANT THAT. I WANT TO DANCE ALL NIGHT. I'VE NEVER KNOWN WHAT IT'S LIKE TO BE IN A WOMAN DANCING."

YES. I DON'T KNOW WHY, BUT I'LL GO TO THE DANCE WITH YOU TONIGHT, TOM.

"FATHER AND MOTHER WOULD NEVER PERMIT IT. DOGS, CATS, LOCUSTS, LEAVES, EVERYTHING ELSE IN THE WORLD AT ONE TIME OR ANOTHER I'VE KNOWN, BUT NEVER A WOMAN IN SPRING, NEVER ON A NIGHT LIKE THIS. OH, PLEASE--WE MUST GO TO THAT DANCE!"

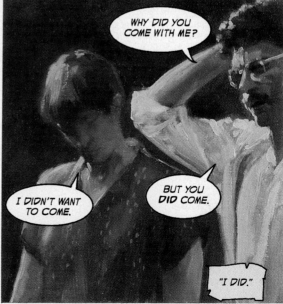

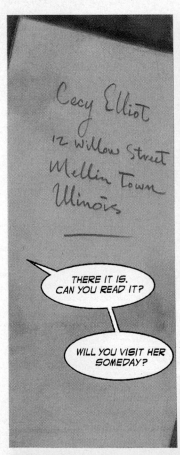

CLARA PECK HAD LIVED IN THE OLD HOUSE FOR TEN YEARS BEFORE SHE MADE THE STRANGE DISCOVERY. SHE HAD MARCHED UP AND DOWNSTAIRS A THOUSAND TIMES, AND NEVER *SEEN.*

IT CAN'T BE! HOW COULD I HAVE BEEN SO BLIND? THERE'S AN *ATTIC* IN MY HOUSE!

Trapdoor

BEFORE LUNCH, SHE FOUND HERSELF STANDING UNDER THE TRAPDOOR AGAIN, HER TOO BRIGHT EYES DARING, FIXING, STARING.

NOW I'VE DISCOVERED THE DAMN THING, WHAT DO I DO WITH IT?

STORAGE ROOM UP THERE I BET. WELL--

AND SHE WENT AWAY, VAGUELY TROUBLED. FEELING HER MIND SLIPPING OFF...

TO HELL WITH THAT, CLARA PECK! YOU'RE ONLY FIFTY-SEVEN. NOT SENILE, YET, BY GOD!

STILL, WHY HADN'T SHE NOTICED?

IT WAS THE SILENCE--THAT WAS IT. HER ROOF HAD NEVER LEAKED, NO WATER HAD EVER TAPPED HER CEILINGS. THE BEAMS NEVER SHIFTED IN THE WIND, AND THERE WERE NO MICE. THE HOUSE HAD STAYED SILENT, AND SHE HAD STAYED BLIND.

SHE WENT TO BED EARLY. IT WAS DURING THAT NIGHT THAT SHE HEARD THE FIRST FAINT TAPPING FROM ABOVE, BEHIND THE BLANK CEILING'S PALE, LUNAR FACE.

MOUSE?

GOING DOWNSTAIRS TO FIX BREAKFAST, SHE FIXED THE TRAPDOOR WITH HER STEADY STARE.

HELL, WHY BOTHER TO LOOK AT AN EMPTY ATTIC? NEXT WEEK, MAYBE.

FOR ABOUT THREE DAYS THE TRAPDOOR VANISHED. THAT IS, SHE FORGOT TO LOOK AT IT, SO IT MIGHT AS WELL NOT HAVE BEEN THERE.

AROUND MIDNIGHT OF THE THIRD NIGHT SHE HEARD THE WHATEVER-THEY-WERE SOUNDS DRIFTING ACROSS HER BEDROOM CEILING.

LYING FLAT IN HER BED, SHE WATCHED THE CEILING SO FIXEDLY SHE FELT SHE COULD X-RAY WHATEVER IT WAS THAT CAVORTED BEHIND THE PLASTER.

A FLEA CIRCUS? A TRIBE OF GYPSY MICE IN EXODUS FROM A NEIGHBOR'S HOUSE? PROBABLY...

THE PATTERNS INCREASED. THE SOFT PROWLINGS BEGAN TO CLUSTER TOWARD AN AREA ABOVE AND BEYOND HER BEDROOM DOOR. SLOWLY, CLARA SAT UP.

SHE PEERED OUT INTO A HALL FLOODED WITH COLD LIGHT FROM A FULL MOON, WHICH POURED THROUGH A LANDING WINDOW TO SHOW HER...

THE TRAPDOOR. AS IF SUMMONED BY HER WARMTH, THE SOUNDS OF THE TINY LOST GHOST FEET RUSHED TO CLUSTER AT THE TRAPDOOR RIM ITSELF.

NO! THEY HEAR ME. THEY WANT ME TO--

THE TRAPDOOR SHUDDERED GENTLY WITH THE TINY ROCKING WEIGHTS OF WHATEVER IT WAS A-RUSTLE THERE. LOUDER, THEN LOUDER STILL...

...WHEN THE PHONE RANG. CLARA FELT A TON OF BLOOD PLUNGE FROM A BROKEN WEIGHT DOWN HER FRAME TO CRUSH HER TOES.

GAH!

RRING

WHO IS IT!?

CLARA! IT'S EMMA CROWLEY! WHAT'S WRONG?

EMMA! YOU SCARED THE HELL OUT OF ME! WHY ARE YOU CALLING THIS LATE?

I COULDN'T SLEEP. I HAD THIS *HUNCH*--ALL OF A SUDDEN I THOUGHT CLARA'S NOT WELL, OR SHE'S HURT...

CLARA SANK TO THE EDGE OF THE BED, THE WEIGHT OF EMMA'S VOICE PULLING HER DOWN.

CLARA, ARE--ARE YOU ALL RIGHT? YOU'RE NOT SICK ARE YOU? THE HOUSE ISN'T ON FIRE, OR ANYTHING?

NO, NO. I'M ALL RIGHT.

THANK GOD. SILLY ME. FORGIVE?

FORGIVEN.

WELL THEN...GOOD NIGHT.

CLARA SAT LOOKING AT THE RECEIVER FOR A FULL MINUTE, AND THEN AT LAST PLACED THE PHONE BLINDLY BACK IN ITS CRADLE.

SHE WENT BACK TO LOOK AT THE TRAPDOOR. IT WAS QUIET.

THINK YOU'RE SMART, *DON'T* YOU?

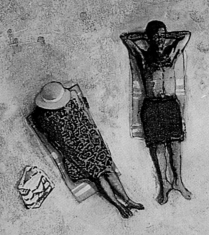

PICASSO SUMMER

GEORGE AND ALICE SMITH DETRAINED AT BIARRITZ
ONE SUMMER NOON, AND IN AN HOUR HAD RUN
THROUGH THEIR HOTEL, ONTO THE BEACH, INTO THE
OCEAN, AND BACK OUT TO BAKE UPON THE SAND.

TO SEE GEORGE SMITH SPRAWLED BURNING
THERE, YOU'D THINK HIM ONLY A TOURIST--
FLOWN FRESH AS ICED LETTUCE TO EUROPE
AND SOON TO BE TRANSSHIPPED HOME.

BUT HERE WAS A MAN WHO LOVED
ART MORE THAN LIFE ITSELF.

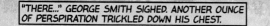
"THERE..." GEORGE SMITH SIGHED. ANOTHER OUNCE OF PERSPIRATION TRICKLED DOWN HIS CHEST.

BOIL OUT THE OHIO TAP WATER, HE THOUGHT, THEN DRINK DOWN THE BEST BORDEAUX. SILT YOUR BLOOD WITH RICH FRENCH SEDIMENT SO YOU'LL SEE WITH NATIVE EYES.

WHY? WHY EAT, BREATHE, DRINK EVERYTHING FRENCH? SO THAT, GIVEN TIME, HE MIGHT REALLY BEGIN TO UNDERSTAND THE GENIUS OF ONE MAN.

HIS MOUTH MOVED, FORMING A NAME.

GEORGE? I KNOW WHAT YOU'VE BEEN THINKING. I CAN READ YOUR LIPS.

AND?

PICASSO.

HE WINCED. SOMEDAY SHE WOULD LEARN TO PRONOUNCE THAT NAME.

PLEASE. RELAX.

ALL RIGHT. PICASSO'S HERE. DOWN THE COAST A FEW MILES AWAY.

BUT YOU MUST FORGET IT OR OUR VACATION'S RUINED.

I WISH I'D NEVER HEARD THE RUMOR.

IF ONLY YOU LIKED OTHER PAINTERS.

OTHERS? YES, THERE WERE OTHERS.

HE COULD BREAKFAST MOST CON-GENIALLY OF CARAVAGGIO'S AUTUMN PEARS AND MIDNIGHT PLUMS. FOR LUNCH: THOSE VAN GOGH SUNFLOWERS, THOSE BLOOMS A BLIND MAN MIGHT READ WITH ONE RUSH OF SCORCHED FINGERS DOWN FIERY CANVAS.

BUT THE GREAT FEAST? WHO ELSE BUT THE CREATOR OF GIRL BEFORE A MIRROR AND GUERNICA?

ALICE, HOW CAN I EXPLAIN?

COMING DOWN THE TRAIN, I THOUGHT, GOOD LORD! IT'S ALL PICASSO COUNTRY!

BUT WAS IT REALLY? HE WONDERED. A MANDOLIN RIPE AS A FRUIT IN SOME MAN'S THOUSAND FINGERPRINTING HANDS, BILLBOARD TATTERS BLOWING LIKE CONFETTI! IN NIGHT WINDS—HOW MUCH WAS PICASSO, HOW MUCH GEORGE SMITH STARING 'ROUND THE WORLD WITH WILD PICASSO EYES?

WOULDN'T IT BE GREAT TO JUST STEP UP TO HIM, SAY "PABLO, HERE'S FIVE THOUSAND! GIVE US THE SEA. THE SAND. THE SKY. OR ANY OLD THING YOU WANT. WE'LL BE HAPPY..."

I THINK YOU'D BETTER GO IN THE WATER NOW.

I KEEP THINKING—IF WE SAVED OUR MONEY...

WE'LL NEVER HAVE FIVE THOUSAND DOLLARS.

I KNOW.

WHITE FIRE SHOWERED UP WHEN HE CUT THE WATER.

DURING THE AFTERNOON GEORGE WENT INTO THE OCEAN. AT LAST, WITH THE SUN'S DECLINE, THEIR BODIES ALL LOBSTER COLORS AND COLORS OF BROILED SQUAB AND GUINEA HEN, THE NOW WARM, NOW COOL PEOPLE TRUDGED FOR THEIR WEDDING-CAKE HOTELS.

THE BEACH LAY DESERTED FOR ENDLESS MILE UPON MILE, SAVE FOR TWO PEOPLE.

ONE WAS GEORGE SMITH, TOWEL OVER SHOULDER, OUT FOR A LAST DEVOTIONAL.

FAR ALONG THE SHORE, ANOTHER SHORTER, SQUARE-CUT MAN WALKED ALONE IN THE TRANQUIL WEATHER. HIS CLOSE-SHAVEN HEAD WAS DYED ALMOST MAHOGANY BY THE SUN, AND HIS EYES WERE CLEAR AND BRIGHT AS WATER.

GLANCING ABOUT, HE SAW THE SUN SLIDING DOWN THE LATE COLORS OF THE DAY, AND THEN, HALF TURNING, SPIED A SMALL WOODEN OBJECT ON THE SAND.

IT WAS NO MORE THAN A SLENDER STICK FROM A LIME ICE CREAM DELICACY LONG SINCE MELTED AWAY.

SMILING, HE PICKED THE STICK UP.

WITH ANOTHER GLANCE AROUND TO REINSURE HIS SOLITUDE, THE MAN STOOPED AGAIN...

...AND, HOLDING THE STICK GENTLY, WITH LIGHT SWEEPS OF HIS HAND, BEGAN TO DO THE ONE THING IN ALL THE WORLD HE KNEW BEST HOW TO DO.

HE BEGAN TO DRAW INCREDIBLE FIGURES ALONG THE SAND.

HE SKETCHED ONE FIGURE AND THEN MOVED OVER AND, STILL LOOKING DOWN, COMPLETELY FOCUSED ON HIS WORK NOW, DREW A SECOND AND A THIRD FIGURE...

A FOURTH...

A FIFTH...

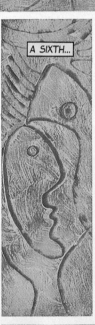

A SIXTH...

AS GEORGE SMITH DREW NEAR, IT WAS OBVIOUS WHAT THE MAN WAS UP TO.

GEORGE SMITH CHUCKLED. OF COURSE, OF COURSE...ALONE ON THE BEACH, THIS MAN—HOW OLD? SIXTY-FIVE? SEVENTY?—WAS SCRIBBLING AND DOODLING AWAY. HOW THE SAND FLEW!

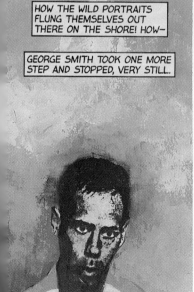

HOW THE WILD PORTRAITS FLUNG THEMSELVES OUT THERE ON THE SHORE! HOW—

GEORGE SMITH TOOK ONE MORE STEP AND STOPPED, VERY STILL.

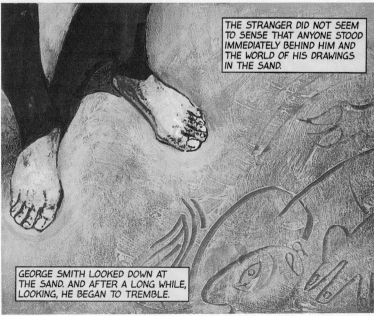

THE STRANGER DID NOT SEEM TO SENSE THAT ANYONE STOOD IMMEDIATELY BEHIND HIM AND THE WORLD OF HIS DRAWINGS IN THE SAND.

GEORGE SMITH LOOKED DOWN AT THE SAND. AND AFTER A LONG WHILE, LOOKING, HE BEGAN TO TREMBLE.

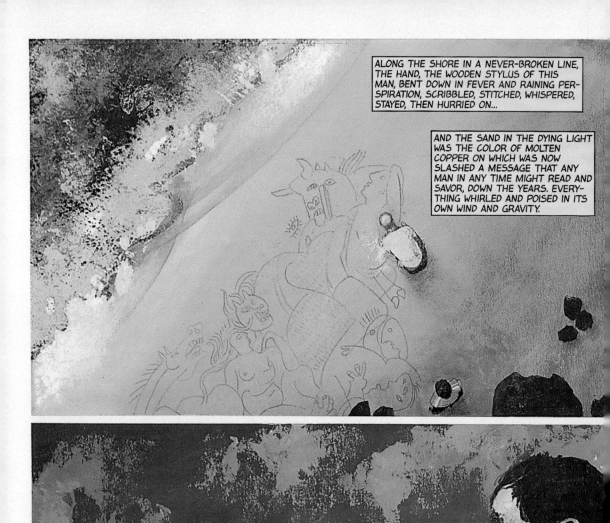

ALONG THE SHORE IN A NEVER-BROKEN LINE, THE HAND, THE WOODEN STYLUS OF THIS MAN, BENT DOWN IN FEVER AND RAINING PERSPIRATION, SCRIBBLED, STITCHED, WHISPERED, STAYED, THEN HURRIED ON...

AND THE SAND IN THE DYING LIGHT WAS THE COLOR OF MOLTEN COPPER ON WHICH WAS NOW SLASHED A MESSAGE THAT ANY MAN IN ANY TIME MIGHT READ AND SAVOR, DOWN THE YEARS. EVERYTHING WHIRLED AND POISED IN ITS OWN WIND AND GRAVITY.

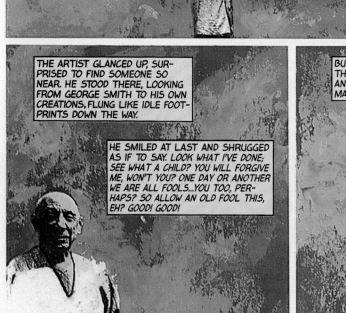

THE ARTIST GLANCED UP, SURPRISED TO FIND SOMEONE SO NEAR. HE STOOD THERE, LOOKING FROM GEORGE SMITH TO HIS OWN CREATIONS, FLUNG LIKE IDLE FOOTPRINTS DOWN THE WAY.

HE SMILED AT LAST AND SHRUGGED AS IF TO SAY: LOOK WHAT I'VE DONE; SEE WHAT A CHILD? YOU WILL FORGIVE ME, WON'T YOU? ONE DAY OR ANOTHER WE ARE ALL FOOLS...YOU TOO, PERHAPS? SO ALLOW AN OLD FOOL THIS, EH? GOOD! GOOD!

BUT GEORGE SMITH COULD ONLY LOOK AT THE LITTLE MAN WITH THE SUN-DARK SKIN AND THE CLEAR SHARP EYES AND SAY THE MAN'S NAME ONCE, IN A WHISPER, TO HIMSELF.

GEORGE WANTED TO RUN BUT DID NOT RUN.

WHAT? GRAB A SHOVEL, DIG, EXCAVATE, SAVE A CHUNK OF THIS ALL-TOO-CRUMBLING SAND? FIND A REPAIRMAN, RACE HIM BACK HERE WITH PLASTER OF PARIS TO CAST A MOLD OF SOME SMALL FRAGILE PART OF THESE?

THE CAMERA! RUN, GET IT, GET BACK, AND HURRY ALONG THE SHORE, CLICKING, CHANGING FILM.

THE SUN BURNED FAINTLY ON HIS FACE. HIS EYES WERE TWO SMALL FIRES FROM IT. THE SUN WAS HALF UNDERWATER, AND AS HE WATCHED, IT SANK THE REST OF THE WAY IN A MATTER OF SECONDS.

THE GREAT ARTIST HAD DRAWN NEARER AND NOW WAS GAZING INTO GEORGE SMITH'S FACE WITH GREAT FRIENDLINESS...

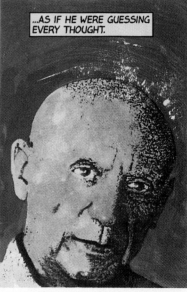

...AS IF HE WERE GUESSING EVERY THOUGHT.

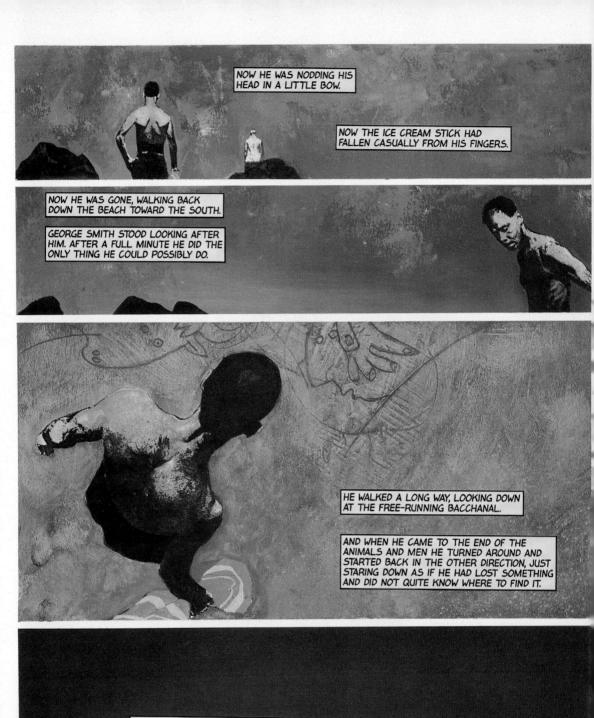

NOW HE WAS NODDING HIS HEAD IN A LITTLE BOW.

NOW THE ICE CREAM STICK HAD FALLEN CASUALLY FROM HIS FINGERS.

NOW HE WAS GONE, WALKING BACK DOWN THE BEACH TOWARD THE SOUTH.

GEORGE SMITH STOOD LOOKING AFTER HIM. AFTER A FULL MINUTE HE DID THE ONLY THING HE COULD POSSIBLY DO.

HE WALKED A LONG WAY, LOOKING DOWN AT THE FREE-RUNNING BACCHANAL.

AND WHEN HE CAME TO THE END OF THE ANIMALS AND MEN HE TURNED AROUND AND STARTED BACK IN THE OTHER DIRECTION, JUST STARING DOWN AS IF HE HAD LOST SOMETHING AND DID NOT QUITE KNOW WHERE TO FIND IT.

HE KEPT ON DOING THIS UNTIL THERE WAS NO MORE LIGHT IN THE SKY OR ON THE SAND TO SEE BY.

RAY BRADBURY

SPECIAL

THE ILLUSTRATED MAN

NANTIER • BEAL • MINOUSTCHINE
publishing inc.
new york

A BYRON PREISS VISUAL PUBLICATIONS, INC. BOOK

INTRODUCTION

"The Illustrated Man" quite obviously derives from my meetings with Mr. Electrico, the carnival magician who, with his Electric Chair, entered my life Labor Day weekend 1932 when I just twelve. Enamored of a man who could have himself electrocuted every night and survive in front of hundreds of customers, I returned one Saturday afternoon to find him seated outside the carnival tent, almost as if he were waiting for me. He asked if I would like to meet the performers of his small carnival. I immediately said yes and he led me inside the tent where I chatted with the Fat Lady, the Human Skeleton, and the Tattooed Man, whom I later relabeled as "illustrated." He had what seemed to be several hundred snakes, lions, kanga-roos, tigers, and pretty ladies stitched in ink all over his good-sized body. Perspiring in the hot sunlight, it almost seemed that his illustrations were dissolving and coming to life.

Remembering this when I was thirty, I wrote the story and it became the front, side, and back of *The Illustrated Man* when it was published forty-two years ago. I made the illustrations move on his flesh to tell stories. Two of them were "The Visitor" and "Zero Hour." "The Visitor" is the work of a boy and man raised in the Baptist Church and wondering if Christ, as promised, would one day have a Second Coming. And what would happen if he arrived on a far planet the day before some astronauts landed? "Zero Hour" is another extension of my childhood. In my twenties, I remembered how brutally honest, and sometimes destructive, boys and girls can be. I let them loose in my story to see what would happen. Now it's *your* turn to find out!

Ray Bradbury

Mark Chiarello's fully painted art can be seen in DC's *Batman/Houdini: The Devil's Workshop* graphic novel and Marvel's *Hellraiser*, as well as the *Stars of the Negro Leagues* (Eclipse), *Star Wars* and Topps's*Dracula* trading card sets. He was recently appointed Color Editor at DC Comics.

Guy Davis is perhaps best known for his work on his Harvey-nominated *Baker Street* series. Recently, he has worked on several projects for DC/Vertigo, including the first story arc for *Sandman Mystery Theater*, written by Matt Wagner, and a *Phantom Stranger* one-shot. Guy is a self-taught artist and lives in Okemos, Michigan.

P. Craig Russell, a twenty-year comics veteran, is known for his adaptations of literary and musical works, including "The Magic Flute," "Salome," Kipling's "Jungle Book" stories, and *Oscar Wilde's Fairy Tales*. Recent works include *Robin 3000*, "Hothouse" for DC's *Legends of the Dark Knight*, and "Ramadan," a *Sandman* story for DC/Vertigo. Russell swept the 1993 comics awards, winning an Inkpot, an Eisner, and a Harvey.

Michael Lark, a talented newcomer, first gained notice for his two collaborations with Debra Rodia, *Airwaves* and *Taken Under*, published by Caliber Press. He is currently working on another Byron Preiss project, an adaptation of Raymond Chandler's *The Little Sister* for the *Raymond Chandler's Philip Marlowe* series, to be published by Marvel Comics.

Jack Kamen started working as a comic book artist in the 1930s with Chesler Studios, which included work on Fawcett's superhero line. After the Second World War, he went to work for Jerry Iger Studios, where he did work for Fiction House's "The Ghost Gallery" in *Jumbo Comics*. Kamen then drew romance books for Harvey Comics until Al Feldstein lured him to EC Comics in 1954. Jack drew for EC's horror and science fiction titles until 1955. He then went into commercial advertising and never looked back. He now lives in comfortable semi-retirement with his wife, splitting their time between New Hampshire and Florida.

Tim Bradstreet is a noted illustrator of role-playing games and comics. Recent work includes *Vampire: A Collection of Dark Portraiture* (White Wolf Game Studio), *Hawkworld* (DC Comics), *Andrew Vachss's Hard Looks* (Dark Horse Comics), and Clive Barker's *Age of Desire* (Eclipse Comics)

Julia Koch began her comics career in 1992 as the art director for Eclipse Comics, working on projects as diverse as *Hot Pulp!*, *True Crime Comics*, and *The Spawn Spogz*. She is now the director of A Virtual Kaliedoscope studio.

Rodney Dunn was born on Norman Rockwell's birthday in 1968. He has worked in TV animation on the *Beetlejuice* animated series, in comics on MISTER X, and in advertising.

Cover by Mark Chiarello
Frontispiece by Tim Bradstreet
Color by Grant Goleash

The Illustrated Man
Adapted by Guy Davis
Lettered by John Workman
Color by Julia Koch

The Visitor
Script & breakdowns by P. Craig Russell
Finished art by Michael Lark
Lettered by John Workman
Color by Michael Lark and Julia Koch

Zero Hour
An EC Classic
Adapted by Jack Kamen
Color by Rodney Dunn

Special thanks to Don Congdon,
Dan Martin at Sprintout,
and Uncle Ray.

Executive Editor: Byron Preiss
Editor: Howard Zimmerman
Art Director/Designer: Dean Motter
Associate Editor: Kenneth Grobe
Managing Editor: Deborah Valcourt

For information address:
Byron Preiss Visual Publications, Inc.
24 West 25th Street, New York, New York 10010.

Printed in Canada.

PROLOGUE

'IT WAS A WARM AFTERNOON IN EARLY SEPTEMBER WHEN I FIRST MET THE ILLUSTRATED MAN. WALKING ALONG AN ASPHALT ROAD, I WAS ON THE FINAL LEG OF A TWO WEEKS' WALKING TOUR OF WISCONSIN.

LATE IN THE AFTERNOON I STOPPED, ATE, AND WAS PREPARING TO STRETCH OUT AND READ WHEN THE ILLUSTRATED MAN WALKED OVER THE HILL.

I DIDN'T KNOW HE WAS ILLUSTRATED THEN, ONLY THAT HE WAS TALL, ONCE WELL-MUSCLED, BUT NOW GOING TO FAT WITH A FACE LIKE A CHILD'S THAT SAT UPON HIS MASSIVE BODY.

DO YOU KNOW WHERE I CAN FIND A JOB?

I'M AFRAID NOT.

I HAVEN'T HAD A JOB THAT'S LASTED IN FORTY YEARS...

WELL, THIS IS AS GOOD A PLACE AS ANY TO SPEND THE NIGHT. DO YOU MIND COMPANY?

NO... NO.

I, UH... HAVE SOME EXTRA FOOD YOU'D BE WELCOME TO.

YOU'LL BE SORRY YOU ASKED ME TO STAY.

EVERYONE ALWAYS IS. THAT'S WHY I'M WALKING. HERE IT IS, EARLY SEPTEMBER, THE CREAM OF THE LABOR DAY CARNIVAL SEASON. I SHOULD BE MAKING MONEY HAND-OVER-FIST AT ANY SMALL-TOWN SIDE-SHOW CELEBRATION. BUT HERE I AM WITH NO PROSPECTS.

I USUALLY KEEP A JOB ABOUT TEN DAYS. THEN SOMETHING HAPPENS AND THEY FIRE ME.

BY NOW, EVERY CARNIVAL IN AMERICA WON'T TOUCH ME WITH A TEN FOOT POLE.

WHAT SEEMS TO BE THE TROUBLE?

FUNNY.

YOU CAN'T FEEL THEM, BUT THEY'RE THERE. I ALWAYS HOPE THAT SOME DAY...

...I'LL LOOK AND THEY'LL BE GONE.

I WALK IN THE SUN FOR HOURS ON THE HOTTEST DAYS, BAKING AND HOPE THAT MY SWEAT'LL WASH THEM OFF, THE SUN'LL COOK THEM OFF, BUT AT SUNDOWN THEY'RE STILL THERE.

ARE THEY STILL THERE NOW?

...YES...

THEY'RE STILL THERE.

THE ILLUSTRATIONS.

ANOTHER REASON I KEEP MY COLLAR BUTTONED UP IS THE CHILDREN. THEY FOLLOW ME ALONG COUNTRY ROADS. EVERYONE WANTS TO SEE THE PICTURES, AND YET NOBODY WANTS TO SEE THEM.

YES...IT KEEPS RIGHT ON GOING.

ALL OF ME IS ILLUSTRATED.

LOOK.

WHY... THEY'RE BEAUTIFUL!

HOW CAN I EXPLAIN ABOUT HIS ILLUSTRATIONS? IF EL GRECO HAD PAINTED MINIATURES IN HIS PRIME, NO BIGGER THAN YOUR HAND, INFINITELY DETAILED, PERHAPS HE MIGHT HAVE USED THIS MAN'S BODY FOR HIS ART.

THE COLORS BURNED IN THREE DIMENSIONS. THEY WERE WINDOWS LOOKING IN UPON FIERY REALITY. THE MAN WAS A WALKING TREASURE GALLERY. THIS WASN'T THE WORK OF A CHEAP CARNIVAL TATTOO MAN WITH THREE COLORS AND WHISKEY ON HIS BREATH. THIS WAS THE ACCOMPLISHMENT OF A LIVING GENIUS...VIBRANT, CLEAR, AND BEAUTIFUL.

OH, YES...I'M SO PROUD OF MY ILLUSTRATIONS THAT I'D LIKE TO BURN THEM OFF. I'VE TRIED SANDPAPER, ACID, A KNIFE...

FOR, YOU SEE, THESE ILLUSTRATIONS PREDICT THE FUTURE.

OH, IT'S ALL RIGHT IN SUNLIGHT. I COULD KEEP A CARNIVAL DAY JOB. BUT AT NIGHT--THE PICTURES MOVE, THE PICTURES CHANGE.

HOW LONG HAVE YOU BEEN ILLUSTRATED?

IN 1900, WHEN I WAS TWENTY YEARS OLD AND WORKING A CARNIVAL, I BROKE MY LEG. IT LAID ME UP; I HAD TO DO SOMETHING TO KEEP MY HAND IN, SO I DECIDED TO GET TATTOOED.

BUT WHO TATTOOED YOU? WHAT HAPPENED TO THE ARTIST?

SHE WENT BACK TO THE FUTURE.

I MEAN IT. SHE WAS AN OLD WOMAN IN A LITTLE HOUSE, A LITTLE OLD WITCH WHO LOOKED A THOUSAND YEARS OLD ONE MOMENT AND TWENTY YEARS OLD THE NEXT.

SHE SAID SHE COULD TRAVEL IN TIME. I LAUGHED. NOW I KNOW BETTER.

I'VE HUNTED EVERY SUMMER FOR FIFTY YEARS...

AND WHEN I FIND THAT WITCH...

I'M GOING TO KILL HER.

THE VISITOR

IT WAS A QUIET MORNING ON MARS, WITH THE DEAD SEA BOTTOM FLAT AND SILENT—NO WIND ON IT. THE SUN WAS CLEAN AND COOL IN THE EMPTY SKY. SAUL WILLIAMS LOOKED WEARILY OUT OF HIS TENT AND THOUGHT ABOUT HOW FAR AWAY EARTH WAS. BUT WHAT COULD YOU DO WHEN YOUR LUNGS WERE FULL OF "BLOOD RUST."

THIS BLOOD RUST—IT FILLED YOUR MOUTH AND YOUR NOSE; IT RAN FROM YOUR EARS, YOUR FINGERNAILS; AND IT TOOK A YEAR TO KILL YOU. THERE WAS NO KNOWN CURE ON EARTH, AND REMAINING WOULD CONTAMINATE AND KILL THE OTHERS.

THE ONLY SOLUTION WAS SHOVING YOU IN A ROCKET AND SHOOTING YOU OUT TO EXILE ON MARS.

SO HERE HE WAS, BLEEDING ALL THE TIME AND FORGOTTEN.

HACK

KAF

KAF

CHRIST, I'M LONELY.

Adapted by P. CRAIG RUSSELL and MICHAEL LARK

HE WANTED VERY MUCH TO BE BACK ON EARTH.

HE TRIED EVERY WAY POSSIBLE TO BE IN NEW YORK CITY.

SOMETIMES, IF HE SAT RIGHT AND HELD HIS HANDS A CERTAIN WAY, HE DID IT. HE COULD ALMOST SMELL NEW YORK.

HELLO, SAUL.

ANOTHER MORNING. I WANT EARTH SO BAD IT HURTS.

IT IS AN AFFLICTION OF THE RUSTED ONES.

THE MAN ON THE BLANKET WAS UNMOVING AND VERY PALE, AS IF HE MIGHT VANISH IF YOU TOUCHED HIM.

I WISH TO GOD THAT YOU COULD AT LEAST TALK. WHY IS IT THAT INTELLECTUALS NEVER GET THE BLOOD RUST AND COME UP HERE?

COME TOMORROW, PERHAPS I'LL HAVE ENOUGH STRENGTH TO TALK ABOUT ARISTOTLE. THEN I'LL TRY. REALLY, I WILL.

I WISH I WERE AS SICK AS YOU. THEN MAYBE I WOULDN'T WORRY ABOUT BEING AN INTELLECTUAL. THEN MAYBE I'D GET SOME PEACE.

YOU'LL GET AS BAD AS I AM NOW IN ABOUT SIX MONTHS. THEN YOU WON'T CARE ABOUT ANYTHING BUT... SLEEP.

SLEEP WILL BE LIKE A WOMAN TO YOU, FRESH, GOOD, AND FAITHFUL.

IT'S A NICE THOUGHT...

SAUL WALKED AWAY.

THE BRIGHT METAL FLASHED ON THE SKY.

A MINUTE LATER, THE ROCKET LANDED ON THE SEA BOTTOM. A MAN STEPPED OUT, CARRYING HIS LUGGAGE. TWO OTHER MEN IN PROTECTIVE GERMICIDE SUITS ACCOMPANIED HIM, BRINGING OUT VAST CASES OF FOOD, SETTING UP A TENT FOR HIM. ANOTHER MINUTE AND THE ROCKET RETURNED TO THE SKY.

SO THIS IS MARS.

HELLO! HELLO!

HELLO. MY NAME'S LEONARD MARK.

I'M SAUL WILLIAMS. HOW'RE THINGS IN NEW YORK?

LIKE THIS.

NEW YORK GREW UP OUT OF THE DESERT, MADE OF STONE AND FILLED WITH MARCH WINDS. NEONS EXPLODED IN ELECTRIC COLOR. YELLOW TAXIS GLIDED IN A STILL NIGHT. BRIDGES ROSE AND TUGS CHANTED IN THE MIDNIGHT HARBORS. CURTAINS ROSE ON SPANGLED MUSICALS.

WHAT'S HAPPENING TO ME? WHAT'S WRONG WITH ME? I'M GOING CRAZY! STOP IT! THIS CAN'T BE!

IT IS.

THE NEW YORK TOWERS FADED. MARS RETURNED. SAUL STOOD ON THE EMPTY SEA BOTTOM, STARING LIMPLY AT THE YOUNG NEWCOMER.

YOU DID IT.

YOU DID IT WITH YOUR MIND.

YES.

OH, BUT I'M GLAD YOU'RE HERE.

YOU CAN'T KNOW HOW GLAD I AM

IT WAS HIGH NOON. THEY HAD BEEN TALKING ALL THROUGH THE WARM MORNING TIME.

AND THIS ABILITY OF YOURS?

IT'S JUST SOMETHING I WAS BORN WITH.

MY MOTHER WAS IN THE BLOWUP OF LONDON IN '57. I WAS BORN TEN MONTHS LATER.

I DON'T KNOW WHAT YOU'D CALL IT. TELEPATHY AND THOUGHT TRANSFERENCE, I SUPPOSE.

I USED TO HAVE AN ACT BACK ON EARTH. MOST PEOPLE THOUGHT I WAS A CHARLATAN.

I DIDN'T LET ANYONE KNOW I WAS REALLY GENUINE, IT WAS SAFER NOT TO LET IT GET AROUND TOO MUCH.

YOU SURE SCARED THE HELL OUT OF ME. WHEN NEW YORK CAME RIGHT UP OUT OF THE GROUND THAT WAY, I THOUGHT I WAS INSANE.

WHAT WOULD YOU LIKE TO BE DOING NOW, MOST OF ALL?

SAUL PUT DOWN HIS CUP. HE TRIED TO HOLD HIS HANDS VERY STEADY.

HE WET HIS LIPS.

I'D LIKE TO BE IN A LITTLE CREEK I USED TO SWIM IN IN MELLINTOWN, ILLINOIS WHEN I WAS A KID.

SAUL FELL BACK ON THE SAND, HIS EYES SHUT. FROM TIME TO TIME, HIS HANDS MOVED, TWITCHING EXCITEDLY.

LEONARD MARK QUIETLY FINISHED HIS COFFEE.

SAUL BEGAN TO MAKE SLOW MOVEMENTS OF HIS ARMS, OUT AND BACK, GASPING WITH HIS HEAD TO ONE SIDE, HIS ARMS COMING AND GOING SLOWLY ON THE WARM AIR, STIRRING THE WARM SAND UNDER HIM, HIS BODY TURNING SLOWLY OVER.

ALL RIGHT.

SAUL SAT UP, RUBBING HIS FACE.

I SAW THE CREEK. I RAN ALONG THE BANK AND I TOOK OFF MY CLOTHES.

AND I DIVED IN AND SWAM AROUND!

I'M PLEASED.

HERE.

THIS IS FOR YOU.

WHAT'S THIS? CHOCOLATE?

NONSENSE, I'M NOT DOING THIS FOR PAY. PUT THAT THING BACK IN YOUR POCKET BEFORE I TURN IT INTO A RATTLING SNAKE AND IT BITES YOU.

THANK YOU. THANK YOU, YOU DON'T KNOW HOW GOOD THAT WATER WAS.

MORE COFFEE? WOULD YOU LIKE MORE COF--

WHAT'S WRONG?

THE OTHER MEN, THE OTHER SICK ONES ALONG THE BOTTOM OF THIS DEAD SEA.

SAUL FELT HIMSELF SWAYING. THE OTHER MEN HAD SEEN THE ROCKET FLASH. NOW THEY WERE COMING TO GREET THE NEW ARRIVAL.

SAUL WAS COLD.

LOOK, MARK... I THINK WE'D BETTER HEAD FOR THE MOUNTAINS.

WHY?

SEE THOSE MEN COMING? SOME OF THEM ARE *INSANE!*

REALLY?

YES!

THEY DON'T LOOK VERY DANGEROUS.

YOU'D BE SUR-PRISED.

YOU'RE TREM-BLING. WHY'S THAT?

DON'T YOU REALIZE THEY'LL FIGHT OVER YOU -- KILL EACH OTHER -- KILL *YOU* FOR THE RIGHT TO OWN YOU? WE HAVEN'T GOT TIME TO ARGUE. *COME ON!*

I'M GOING TO SIT RIGHT HERE UNTIL THOSE MEN SHOW UP. YOU'RE TOO POSSESSIVE. MY LIFE'S MY OWN.

YOU HEARD ME.

IT'S A *LIE!* FOR GOD'S SAKE... DON'T, MARK! THE MEN ARE COMING! YOU'LL BE KILLED!

LET THEM COME. I CAN FOOL THEM ALL.

NO!

WHEN NEW YORK WAS GONE, THERE WAS ONLY THE WIDE SOUNDLESSNESS OF THE DEAD SEA.

THE MEN WERE CLOSING IN AROUND HIM. HE HEADED FOR THE HILLS WITH HIS PRECIOUS CARGO, WITH NEW YORK AND GREEN COUNTRY AND FRESH SPRINGS AND OLD FRIENDS HELD IN HIS ARMS.

HE DID NOT STOP RUNNING.

NIGHT FILLED THE CAVE...

I'LL UNTIE YOU IF YOU PROMISE NOT TO RUN AWAY.

I COULDN'T PROMISE THAT. I'M A FREE AGENT. I DON'T BELONG TO ANYBODY.

BUT YOU'VE *GOT* TO BELONG. I CAN'T LET YOU GO AWAY.

THE MORE YOU SAY THINGS LIKE THAT, THE MORE REMOTE I AM. IF YOU'D DONE THINGS INTELLIGENTLY, WE'D HAVE BEEN FRIENDS.

I'M SORRY, BUT I KNOW THOSE MEN TOO WELL!

ARE YOU ANY DIFFERENT? HARDLY. GO OUT AND SEE IF THEY'RE COMING.

I THOUGHT I HEARD A NOISE.

SAUL RAN. IN THE CAVE ENTRANCE, PEERING DOWN INTO THE NIGHT-FILLED GULLY...

I DON'T SEE ANY-THING. I...

MARK!

MARK WAS GONE.

MARK! MARK! COME BACK!

STOP!

THE BOULDER VANISHED. MARK WAS THERE.

IT DIDN'T WORK.

IF YOU KILL ME, WHERE WILL YOUR DREAMS BE? GO AHEAD ...KILL ME. I DARE YOU!

SHADOWS MOVED INTO THE CAVE MOUTH. THE OTHER MEN WERE THERE.

GOOD EVENING. COME IN, GENTLEMEN.

BY DAWN, THE ARGUMENTS AND FEROCITIES STILL CONTINUED. MARK HAD CREATED A MAHOGANY-PANELED CONFERENCE HALL AND A MARBLE TABLE AT WHICH THEY ALL SAT, RIDICULOUSLY BEARDED, EVIL-SMELLING, SWEATY AND GREEDY MEN, EYES BENT UPON THEIR TREASURE.

THE WAY TO SETTLE IT IS FOR EACH OF YOU TO HAVE CERTAIN HOURS OF CERTAIN DAYS. I'LL TREAT YOU ALL EQUALLY. LET'S SEE, NOW...

ON MONDAYS, SMITH, ON TUESDAYS, I'LL TAKE PETER AND I'LL FINISH WITH JOHNSON, HOLTZMAN, AND JIM ON WEDNESDAYS.

AS FOR SAUL, HE'S ON PROBATION UNTIL HE'S PROVED HE CAN BE A CIVIL PERSON ONCE MORE.

UNTIL THAT TIME, I'LL HAVE NOTHING TO DO WITH HIM.

THE REST OF THE WEEK, I'M TO BE LEFT STRICTLY ALONE. IF YOU DON'T OBEY, I WON'T PERFORM AT ALL.

MAYBE WE'LL **MAKE** YOU PERFORM.

LOOK, WE'RE FIVE AGAINST HIS ONE. WE CAN MAKE HIM DO ANYTHING WE WANT.

DON'T BE IDIOTS.

HE'S TELLING US WHAT HE'LL DO. WHY DON'T WE TELL **HIM?** ARE WE BIGGER THAN HIM, OR NOT?

DON'T LISTEN TO HIM. HE'S CRAZY. YOU KNOW WHAT HE'LL DO, DON'T YOU?

HE'LL GET YOU ALL OFF-GUARD AND KILL YOU ONE BY ONE.

AND TO MAKE MATTERS WORSE, **ONE OF YOU** HAS A GUN!

SEARCH! FIND THE ONE WITH THE GUN OR YOU'RE ALL **DEAD!**

THAT DID IT.

JOHNSON FELL BACK, FEELING IN HIS JACKET.

ALL RIGHT, HERE. YOU... SMITH.

BANG

BANG BANG

STOP!

LOOK, YOU FOOLS!

NEW YORK SOARED UP AROUND THEM OUT OF ROCK AND CAVE AND SKY. SUN GLINTED ON HIGH TOWERS, THE ELEVATED THUNDERED; TUGS BLEW IN THE HARBOR. AND, IN THE CENTER OF NEW YORK, BEWILDERED, THE MEN STUMBLED.

BANG BANG BANG BANG

SAUL RAN FORWARD...

...CRASHED AGAINST JOHNSON...

...GRAPPLED FOR THE GUN.

IT FIRED AGAIN.

BANG

THEY STOOD. THEY CEASED STRUGGLING. THERE WAS A TERRIBLE SILENCE.

NEW YORK SANK DOWN INTO THE SEA WITH A HISSING, BUBBLING, SIGHING; WITH A CRY OF RUINED METAL AND OLD TIME, THE GREAT STRUCTURES LEANED, WARPED, FLOWED, COLLAPSED.

MARK STOOD AMONG THE BUILDINGS. THEN, LIKE A BUILDING

--A NEAT, RED HOLE DRILLED INTO HIS CHEST--

WORDLESS, HE FELL.

LEONARD!

LEONARD?

LEONARD.

LEONARD MARK DID NOT MOVE. HIS EYES WERE SHUT. HIS CHEST HAD CEASED GOING UP AND DOWN.

HE WAS GETTING COLD.

THE ONLY ONE WE DIDN'T WANT TO KILL... WE KILLED.

GET A SPADE. BURY HIM.

I'LL HAVE NOTHING TO DO WITH YOU.

THERE WAS THE SOUND OF SOMEONE DIGGING IN THE EARTH. "WE DON'T NEED HIM, ANYHOW," SAID SOMEBODY, MUCH TOO LOUDLY.

SLEEP. WE'LL ALL GO TO SLEEP NOW. WE HAVE THAT MUCH, ANYWAY. GO TO SLEEP AND TRY TO DREAM OF NEW YORK AND ALL THE REST.

HE CLOSED HIS EYES WEARILY, THE BLOOD GATHERING IN HIS NOSE AND HIS MOUTH AND IN HIS QUIVERING EYES.

HOW DID HE DO IT? HOW DID HE BRING NEW YORK UP HERE AND MAKE US WALK AROUND IN IT?

LET'S TRY. IT SHOULDN'T BE TOO HARD. **THINK!** THINK OF NEW YORK AND CENTRAL PARK AND THEN ILLINOIS IN THE SPRING. APPLE BLOSSOMS AND GREEN GRASS.

IT DIDN'T WORK. IT WASN'T THE SAME. NEW YORK WAS GONE AND NOTHING HE COULD DO WOULD BRING IT BACK. HE WOULD RISE EVERY MORNING AND WALK ON THE DEAD SEA LOOKING FOR IT... AND NEVER FIND IT.

AND FINALLY LIE, TOO TIRED TO WALK, TRYING TO FIND NEW YORK IN HIS HEAD, BUT NOT FINDING IT.

THE LAST THING HE HEARD BEFORE HE SLEPT WAS THE SPADE RISING AND FALLING AND DIGGING A HOLE INTO WHICH...

WITH A TREMENDOUS CRASH OF METAL AND GOLDEN MIST AND ODOR AND COLOR AND SOUND...

NEW YORK COLLAPSED, FELL, AND WAS BURIED.

EACH ILLUSTRATION IS A LITTLE STORY. IF YOU WATCH THEM, IN A FEW MINUTES THEY TELL YOU A TALE.

SO PEOPLE FIRE ME WHEN MY PICTURES MOVE. THEY DON'T LIKE IT WHEN VIOLENT THINGS HAPPEN IN MY ILLUSTRATIONS.

IN THREE HOURS OF LOOKING, YOU COULD SEE EIGHTEEN OR TWENTY STORIES ACTED RIGHT ON MY BODY. YOU COULD HEAR VOICES AND THINK THOUGHTS.

IT'S ALL HERE, JUST WAITING FOR YOU TO LOOK. BUT MOST OF ALL, THERE'S A SPECIAL SPOT ON MY BODY.

SEE? THERE'S NO SPECIAL DESIGN, JUST A JUMBLE.

WHEN I'VE BEEN AROUND A PERSON LONG ENOUGH, THAT SPOT CLOUDS OVER AND FILLS IN. IF I'M WITH A WOMAN, HER PICTURE COMES THERE ON MY BACK IN AN HOUR AND SHOWS HER WHOLE LIFE-- HOW SHE'LL LIVE, HOW SHE'LL DIE, WHAT SHE'LL LOOK LIKE WHEN SHE'S SIXTY.

AND IF IT'S A MAN, AN HOUR LATER HIS PICTURE'S HERE ON MY BACK, SHOWING HIM FALLING OFF A CLIFF OR DYING UNDER A TRAIN. SO I'M FIRED AGAIN.

THEY'RE MOVING, AREN'T THEY?

...YES...

THE PICTURES WERE MOVING, EACH IN ITS TURN, EACH FOR A BRIEF MOMENT OR TWO. MY EYES FOCUSED UPON A SCENE...

...A LARGE HOUSE, A GREEN LAWN, CHILDREN AT PLAY. THE ILLUSTRATION BEGAN TO QUIVER...

...AND CAME TO LIFE.

ZERO HOUR

IT WAS AN INTERESTING FACT THAT THE FURY AND BUSTLE OCCURRED ONLY AMONG THE YOUNGER CHILDREN. THE OLDER ONES, THOSE TEN YEARS AND MORE, DISDAINED THE AFFAIR AND MARCHED SCORNFULLY OFF ON HIKES, OR PLAYED A MORE DIGNIFIED GAME OF HIDE AND SEEK ON THEIR OWN. MEANWHILE, PARENTS CAME AND WENT IN CHROMIUM BEETLE CARS. REPAIRMEN CAME TO REPAIR VACUUM ELEVATORS IN HOUSES, TO FIX FLUTTERING TELEVISION SETS, OR HAMMER UPON STUBBORN FOOD-DELIVERY TUBES. THE ADULT CIVILIZATION PASSED AND REPASSED THE BUSY YOUNGSTERS... IGNORING THEM...

THIS... AND THIS... AND *THIS*. DO THAT, AND BRING *THAT* OVER HERE. NO! *HERE*, NINNY! RIGHT. NOW, GET BACK WHILE I FIX THIS. THERE! SEE?

THE CHILDREN CATAPULTED ACROSS GREEN LAWNS, SHOUTING AT EACH OTHER. MINK RAN INTO HER HOUSE, ALL DIRT AND SWEAT...

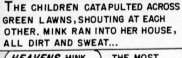

HEAVENS, MINK, WHAT'S GOING ON?

THE MOST *EXCITING* GAME EVER!

FOR HER SEVEN YEARS, MINK WAS LOUD AND STRONG AND DEFINITE! HER MOTHER, MRS. MORRIS, WATCHED HER AS SHE YANKED OUT DRAWERS AND RATTLED PANS AND TOOLS INTO A LARGE SACK...

STOP AND GET YOUR *BREATH*.

I'M ALL RIGHT! OKAY IF I *TAKE* THESE THINGS, MOM?

ALL RIGHT! BUT DON'T *DENT* THEM. ER... WHAT'S THE *NAME* OF THE GAME, DEAR?

INVASION!

1

IN ALMOST EVERY YARD ON THE STREET, CHILDREN BROUGHT OUT KNIVES AND FORKS AND POKERS AND OLD STOVEPIPES AND CAN OPENERS...

I WANNA *PLAY.*

GO *AWAY.* YOU'D JUST MAKE *FUN* OF US.

TWELVE-YEAR-OLD JOSEPH CONNERS SURVEYED THE YOUNGER CHILDREN WITH RELUCTANCE AND A CERTAIN WISTFULNESS...

HONEST, I *WOULDN'T* MAKE FUN. *LET* ME PLAY...

YOU'RE *TOO OLD.* YOU'D ONLY *LAUGH* AND *SPOIL THE INVASION.*

JOSEPH WALKED OFF SLOWLY. HE KEPT LOOKING BACK, ALL DOWN THE BLOCK. MINK TALKED EARNESTLY TO SOMEONE NEAR THE ROSE BUSH...THOUGH *THERE WAS NO ONE THERE.* ANNA TOOK NOTES ON A PAD...

TRIANGLE!

HUH? HOW DO YOU *SPELL* IT?

MINK'S MOTHER, FROM HER UPSTAIRS WINDOW, GAZED DOWN...

T-R-I-...OH, SPELL IT *YOURSELF!* NOW...*BEAM!*

I STILL HAVEN'T GOT TRI... ANGLE DOWN YET!

A-N-G-L-E, ANNA!

OH, *THANKS,* MRS. MORRIS!

THAT'S *ALL RIGHT,* ANNA!

NOW...*BEAM!* THEN...FOUR-NINE-SEVEN-A-AND-B-AND -X...

MINK'S MOTHER WITHDREW, LAUGHING, TO DUST THE HALL WITH AN ELECTRO-DUSTER MAGNET...

...AND A FORK... AND A STRING... AND A HEX... HEX... HEX A GONY... *HEXAGONAL!*

AT LUNCH, MINK GULPED MILK AT ONE TOSS AND WAS AT THE DOOR. MRS. MORRIS SLAPPED THE TABLE...

YOU SIT RIGHT BACK DOWN AND FINISH...

BUT MOM! DRILL'S WAITING FOR ME!

DRILL? WHAT A PECULIAR NAME? WHO'S DRILL?

YOU DON'T KNOW HIM, MOM. YOU'LL MAKE *FUN.* EVERYBODY POKES FUN. GEE, DARN. I GOT TO RUN IF WE WANT TO HAVE THE *INVASION!*

WHO'S INVADING *WHAT?*

MARTIANS... INVADING EARTH!

2

AT FOUR O'CLOCK, THE AUDIO-VISOR BUZZED. MARY MORRIS FLIPPED THE TAB AND THE SCREEN LIT UP...

HELLO, HELEN! THIS *IS* A SURPRISE! HOW ARE THINGS IN *NEW YORK?* YOU LOOK *TIRED!*

HELLO, MARY. I *AM* TIRED. THE CHILDREN. UNDERFOOT...

MY MINK, TOO. THE *SUPER-INVASION!*

ARE *YOUR* KIDS PLAYING THAT GAME TOO?

LORD, *YES.* WERE *WE* THIS BAD WHEN *WE* WERE KIDS, HELEN?

WORSE. DON'T KNOW HOW *MY* PARENTS PUT *UP* WITH ME. I GUESS PARENTS LEARN TO *SHUT THEIR EARS!*

A SILENCE...

WHAT'S *WRONG,* MARY?

EH? OH, NOTHING. JUST THINKING... ABOUT *SHUTTING EARS* AND SUCH. NEVER MIND. WHERE *WERE* WE?

MY BOY *TIM'S* GOT A CRUSH ON SOME GUY NAMED... *DRILL,* I THINK IT IS!

MUST BE A NEW *PASS-WORD.* MINK LIKES HIM *TOO.*

DIDN'T KNOW IT HAD *GOTTEN* AS FAR SOUTH AS *PHILADELPHIA,* MARY! I TALKED TO MY SISTER IN *BOSTON* AND *SHE* SAID HER KIDS ARE *WILD* ABOUT THIS NEW GAME!

IT... IT MUST BE *SWEEP-ING* THE... *COUNTRY!*

AT THIS MOMENT MINK TROTTED INTO THE KITCHEN. MARY MORRIS TURNED FROM THE AUDIO-VISOR...

WHAT'S THAT YOU HAVE THERE, MINK?

A YO-YO, MOM. WATCH.

MINK FLUNG THE YO-YO DOWN ITS STRING. REACHING THE END, IT... VANISHED...

SEE?

GASP...

DIBBLING HER FINGER, MINK MADE THE YO-YO REAPPEAR AND ZIP UP THE STRING...

D-DO THAT AGAIN!

CAN'T! ZERO HOUR'S FIVE O'CLOCK! 'BYE!

4

ON THE AUDIO-VISOR HELEN LAUGHED...

TIM BROUGHT ONE OF THOSE YO-YOS IN THIS MORNING, MARY. WHEN I GOT *CURIOUS*, HE SAID HE WOULDN'T *SHOW* IT TO ME. AND WHEN *I TRIED* TO WORK IT, FINALLY, IT *WOULDN'T* WORK!

MRS. MORRIS WHISPERED...

YOU'RE...NOT *IMPRESSIONABLE,* HELEN!

WHAT?

NEVER MIND. SOMETHING I *THOUGHT* OF. CAN I *HELP* YOU, HELEN?

I WANTED TO GET THAT BLACK AND WHITE CAKE RECIPE...

THE HOUR DROWSED BY. THE DAY WANED. THE SUN LOWERED IN THE PEACEFUL BLUE SKY. ONE LITTLE GIRL RAN OFF CRYING...

MINK, WAS THAT PEGGY ANN CRYING?

YEAH. SHE'S A SCAREBABY. WE WON'T LET HER PLAY, NOW. SHE'S GETTING TOO OLD TO PLAY.

MINK WAS BENT OVER IN THE YARD NEAR THE ROSE BUSH...

I GUESS SHE *GREW UP* ALL OF A SUDDEN.

MINK! DID YOU *HIT* PEGGY ANN?

NO. HONEST. YOU ASK HER. IT WAS SOMETHING... WELL, SHE'S JUST A SCAREDY PANTS. GOLLY. *GOLLY!*

WHAT'S WRONG?

THE RING OF CHILDREN DREW IN AROUND MINK WHERE SHE SCOWLED AT HER WORK WITH SPOONS AND A KIND OF SQUARE-SHAPED ARRANGEMENT OF HAMMERS AND PIPES...

DRILL'S *STUCK* HALF-WAY.

HALF-WAY?

IF WE COULD ONLY GET HIM *ALL* THE WAY THROUGH, IT'D BE *EASIER.* THEN ALL THE *OTHERS* COULD COME THROUGH *AFTER* HIM!

CAN I... *HELP?*

NO'M, THANKS. I'LL FIX IT.

ALL RIGHT, DEAR. HALF AN HOUR MORE. THEN BATH-TIME...

5

MRS. MORRIS WENT BACK INSIDE. TIME PASSED. A CURIOUS, WAITING SILENCE CAME UPON THE STREET, DEEPENING...

FIVE O'CLOCK...FIVE O'CLOCK. TIME'S A-WASTING. FIVE O'CLOCK...

THE VOICE-CLOCK SANG SOFTLY IN A QUIET MUSICAL VOICE, THEN PURRED AWAY IN SILENCE. MRS. MORRIS CHUCKLED IN HER THROAT...

ZERO...HOUR...

MR. MORRIS'S BEETLE CAR HUMMED INTO THE DRIVEWAY. HE GOT OUT, STOOD FOR A MOMENT WATCHING THE CHILDREN, THEN CAME INSIDE...

HELLO, DARLING.

HELLO, HENRY.

MRS. MORRIS LISTENED. THE CHILDREN WERE SILENT...TOO SILENT. MR. MORRIS EMPTIED HIS PIPE...

SWELL DAY. MAKES YOU GLAD TO BE ALIVE.

WHAT'S THAT?

A BUZZING SOUND...MARY GOT UP SUDDENLY, HER EYES WIDENING...

THOSE CHILDREN HAVEN'T ANYTHING DANGEROUS OUT THERE, HAVE THEY?

NOTHING BUT PIPES AND HAMMERS. WHY?

THE BUZZING CONTINUED...

NOTHING ELECTRICAL?

HECK, NO! I LOOKED.

JUST THE SAME, YOU'D BETTER TELL THEM TO QUIT. IT'S AFTER FIVE. TELL THEM...HEH, HEH... TELL THEM TO PUT OFF THEIR INVASION UNTIL TOMORROW...

THE BUZZING GREW LOUDER...

SAY! WHAT ARE THEY UP TO? I'D BETTER GO LOOK...

THE EXPLOSION...

6

THE HOUSE SHOOK WITH A DULL SOUND. THERE WERE OTHER EXPLOSIONS IN OTHER YARDS ON OTHER STREETS...

UP THIS WAY! IN THE ATTIC!

IT'S *NOT UP THERE!* IT'S *OUTSIDE!*

THERE WAS NO TIME TO ARGUE WITH HENRY. LET HIM THINK HER INSANE! SHRIEKING, SHE RAN UPSTAIRS...

I'LL *SHOW* YOU! HURRY! HURRY! I'LL *SHOW* YOU!

MARY!

ANOTHER EXPLOSION OUTSIDE. THE CHILDREN SCREAMED WITH DELIGHT AS IF AT A GREAT FIREWORKS DISPLAY. HENRY RAN AFTER MARY...UP INTO THE ATTIC...

THERE, THERE. WE'RE *SAFE* UNTIL *TONIGHT!* MAYBE WE CAN *SNEAK OUT.* MAYBE WE CAN *ESCAPE.*

ARE YOU *CRAZY,* MARY? WHAT'S GOT *INTO* YOU?

SHE WAS BABBLING WILD STUFF NOW. IT CAME OUT OF HER. ALL THE SUBCONSCIOUS SUSPICIONS AND FEAR. SHE SLAMMED THE DOOR...LOCKED IT...FLUNG THE KEY INTO A FAR, CLUTTERED CORNER...

WHY'D YOU THROW THE *KEY* AWAY, MARY?

QUIET! THEY WILL HEAR US. OH, GOD, THEY'LL FIND US SOON ENOUGH...

BELOW THEM, MINK'S VOICE. THEN FOOTSTEPS CAME INTO THE HOUSE. HEAVY FOOTSTEPS...

WHO'S THAT TRAMPING AROUND DOWN THERE?

MOM? DAD? WHERE ARE YOU?

HEAVY FEET. TWENTY, THIRTY, FORTY OF THEM...

WHO'S DOWNSTAIRS?

HUSH, HENRY! OH, NONONONO! PLEASE BE *QUIET!* THEY MIGHT GO *AWAY!*

HEAVY, VERY HEAVY FOOTSTEPS CAME UP THE STAIRS. MINK LEADING THEM. THEY TREMBLED TOGETHER IN SILENCE IN THE ATTIC, MR. AND MRS. MORRIS. THEY STOOD SHIVERING IN THE DARK SILENCE...

MOM? DAD?

A LITTLE HUMMING SOUND, THE ATTIC LOCK MELTED. THE DOOR OPENED. MINK PEERED INSIDE...TALL BLUE SHADOWS BEHIND HER...

PEEKABOO!

7

EPILOGUE

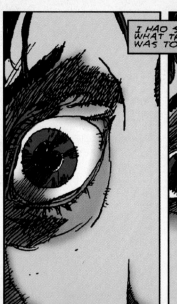

I HAD SEEN WHAT THERE WAS TO SEE.

THE STORIES WERE TOLD; THEY WERE OVER AND DONE.

THERE REMAINED ONLY THAT EMPTY SPACE UPON THE ILLUSTRATED MAN'S BACK. THAT AREA OF JUMBLED COLORS AND SHAPES.

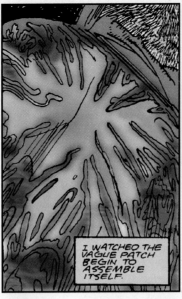

I WATCHED THE VAGUE PATCH BEGIN TO ASSEMBLE ITSELF.

SLOWLY DIS-SOLVING FROM ONE SHAPE TO ANOTHER.

AND STILL ANOTHER.

AT LAST A FACE FORMED ITSELF THERE, A FACE THAT GAZED OUT AT ME FROM THE COLORED FLESH.

A FACE WITH A FAMILIAR NOSE AND MOUTH, FAMILIAR EYES.

I RAN DOWN THE ROAD IN THE MOONLIGHT. I DIDN'T LOOK BACK.

A SMALL TOWN LAY AHEAD, DARK AND ASLEEP. I KNEW THAT, LONG BEFORE MORNING, I WOULD REACH THE TOWN...